They Are All my Favourite Books

An Ivy and Mack story

Written by Rebecca Colby

Illustrated by Gustavo Mazali

with Alicia Arlandis

Collins

What's in this story?

Listen and say

parrot

castle

Download the audio at www.collins.co.uk/839666

penguin

dragon

alien

crocodile

pineapple

🎧 It was story time at the bookshop. Grandpa took Ivy and Mack to 'Meet the Writer'.

Ivy pointed at the poster. "I love Anna Green's books!"

4

Ivy and Mack looked at the bookshelves.
There were tall books, short books,
fat books and thin books.

"Which is your favourite?" asked Ivy.

"I don't know," answered Mack. "They are
all my favourite books!"

It was time to 'Meet the Writer'.
Anna Green said, "Hello," to all the
children and smiled.

"Hello, everyone! Thank you for coming today! Now … who likes writing stories?" asked Anna Green.

Ivy and Mack put up their hands.

"Fantastic! Would you both like to come here?"

Ivy and Mack stood next to Anna Green. "What are your names?"

"I'm Ivy," said Ivy. "And this is my brother, Mack."

"Hello, Ivy and Mack. I'm Anna. Let's tell a story!"

"Now, let's start," said Anna. "Stories need a 'Who?' 'Where?' and 'What?' "

"I know!" said Ivy. "The 'Who' is an alien!"

"That's a good idea," said Anna. "I like writing about aliens!"

Then Anna asked Mack, "And *where* is the story, Mack?"

Mack said, "In a castle! The alien is very important and lives in a castle."

Anna drew an alien and a castle. "And, *what* does the alien do in this story?" said Anna.

"The alien has a birthday party," said Mack. "All his friends come."

"That's very good!" said Anna. "And who are his friends, Ivy?"

"A dragon, a penguin and a parrot!"
said Ivy. "They eat all the food!"

"Then the alien's best friend, Croc, comes to the party. He eats some pineapple. And he … ," said Mack.

Ivy helped with his story. "The crocodile eats the alien's shoes!" she said.

All the children laughed. "That's a GREAT story!" said Anna.

"Let's finish the story now," said Anna.
"What do they do at the end?"

"It's home time," said Mack.

"They all go home," said Ivy.

Anna drew a picture of the animals in a very long car. "Thank you! That is a great story and you're both very good writers!"

Ivy and Mack stood in a line. "You can both buy one of Anna Green's books," said Grandpa.

They got to the table but there were no more books.

"I'm very sorry," said Anna. She stood up. "Wait here!" she said.

Anna came back with a big book.
"You wrote a very good story and I want you to take it home," she said.

She gave the book to Ivy and Mack.

"Thank you very much!" said Ivy. "There are lots of books in this bookshop …"

"But *this* is our favourite book!" said Mack.

THE ALIEN'S BIRTHDAY PARTY
By IVY and MACK
with ANNA GREEN

Picture dictionary

Listen and repeat

bookshelves

bookshop

next to

poster

writer

1 Look and order the story

2 Listen and say

Collins

Published by Collins
An imprint of HarperCollins*Publishers*
Westerhill Road
Bishopbriggs
Glasgow
G64 2QT

HarperCollins*Publishers*
1st Floor, Watermarque Building
Ringsend Road
Dublin 4
Ireland

William Collins' dream of knowledge for all began with the publication of his first book in 1819.

A self-educated mill worker, he not only enriched millions of lives, but also founded a flourishing publishing house. Today, staying true to this spirit, Collins books are packed with inspiration, innovation and practical expertise. They place you at the centre of a world of possibility and give you exactly what you need to explore it.

© HarperCollins*Publishers* Limited 2020

10 9 8 7 6 5 4 3 2

ISBN 978-0-00-839666-4

www.collins.co.uk/elt

British Library Cataloguing in Publication Data

A catalogue record for this publication is available from the British Library.

Author: Rebecca Colby
Lead illustrator: Gustavo Mazali (Beehive)
Copy illustrator: Alicia Arlandis (Beehive)
Series editor: Rebecca Adlard
Commissioning editor: Zoë Clarke
Publishing manager: Lisa Todd
Product managers: Jennifer Hall and Caroline Green
In-house editor: Alma Puts Keren
Project manager: Emily Hooton
Editor: Deborah Friedland
Proofreaders: Natalie Murray and Michael Lamb
Cover designer: Kevin Robbins
Typesetter: 2Hoots Publishing Services Ltd
Audio produced by id audio, London
Reading guide author: Julie Penn
Production controller: Rachel Weaver
Printed and bound by: GPS Group, Slovenia

MIX
Paper from
responsible sources
FSC
www.fsc.org
FSC™ C007454

Download the audio for this book and a reading guide
for parents and teachers at www.collins.co.uk/839666